For Grandpa.

David Mack Shuter — May 4, 1921–May 3, 1994
9th Canadian Armoured Regiment,
British Columbia Dragoons
Aboriginal War Veteran, WWII — N.I.C.

For Madison Leigh and Louise — K.L.

GLOSSARY

Nɬəʔkepmxcin: Language spoken by Interior Salish peoples.
 Also known as Thompson.
schmém'iʔt: Kids.
yuxkn: Small log building with a dirt roof.

Text copyright © 2011 by Nicola I. Campbell
Illustrations copyright © 2011 by Kim LaFave
Published in Canada and the USA in 2011 by Groundwood Books
Third printing 2020

Groundwood Books / House of Anansi Press
groundwoodbooks.com

We gratefully acknowledge for their financial support of our
publishing program the Canada Council for the Arts, the Ontario
Arts Council and the Government of Canada.

Library and Archives Canada Cataloguing in Publication

Campbell, Nicola I.
Grandpa's girls / Nicola I. Campbell ; Kim LaFave, illustrator.

ISBN 978-1-55498-084-0

I. LaFave, Kim II. Title.

PS8605.A5475G73 2011   jC813'.6   C2011-901135-2

Design by Michael Solomon
Printed and bound in China

A NOTE ON THE ART
Ink drawings were scanned into the computer and then color
was applied digitally.

Canada Council   Conseil des Arts
for the Arts   du Canada

ONTARIO ARTS COUNCIL
CONSEIL DES ARTS DE L'ONTARIO
an Ontario government agency
un organisme du gouvernement de l'Ontario

With the participation of the Government of Canada
Avec la participation du gouvernement du Canada | Canada

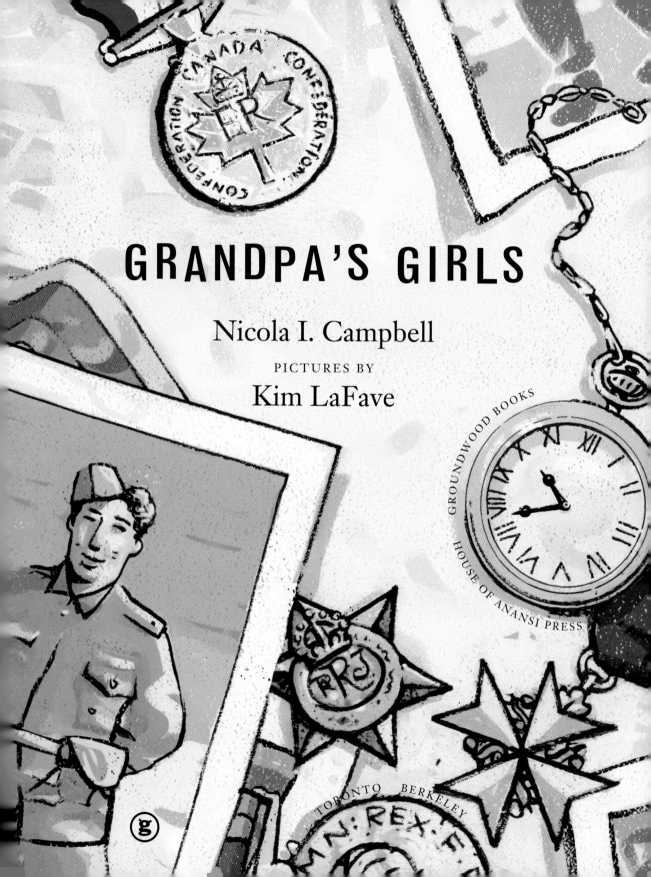

GRANDPA'S GIRLS

Nicola I. Campbell

PICTURES BY

Kim LaFave

GROUNDWOOD BOOKS

HOUSE OF ANANSI PRESS

TORONTO   BERKELEY

"ALL RIGHT, get your things.
We're going to Grandpa's house."

My mom doesn't have to tell me twice.
Just like that, I jump into the car.

My grandpa's house is small, blue
and right beside Highway 5.
Grandpa is a veteran, a cowboy,
a rancher and a businessman.
When he was young
he traveled to Europe
and fought in World War II.

Grandpa has twelve brothers and sisters.
Most of them live near the fresh-water springs
    and grow huge gardens and hay fields,
      where the horses and cows graze.

Our grand-aunties and grand-uncles call us kids *schmém'iʔt* and talk in *Nɬəʔkepmxcin*. Most of it we don't understand, but we always try.

My cousins and I play everywhere.
From Grandpa's house we run
through the field, then stop
beside the highway.

"Remember to look both ways
before you cross that highway!"

Grandpa is standing on the porch
and he watches as we run across.

The *yuxkn* is a small log building.
The roof is covered with dirt and leaves.
It is beside my great-grandparents' house.
It's a storage shed now, but a long time ago
my grand-auntie lived there with her *schmém'i?t*.

By the *yuxkn* and the chicken coop
we play among the chickens,
and pine needles gather in our hair.

The root cellar is like a pit house.
It is halfway underground and
has its own wooden door.
This is where we play house.

We inspect the potatoes
and dust-covered jars of tomatoes,
cherries, huckleberries and sockeye salmon
on shelves that line the dirt walls,
from dirt floor to cobweb-covered ceiling.

Surrounded by the sweet
scent of hay and oats,
we swing on a braided rope,
through the loft and out the window
of Grandpa's big red barn.

"Be careful up there," he calls.

Grandpa is in his toolshed.
It's dark inside and smells like oil and leather —
bridles, saddles, stirrups,
a tractor and power tools.

"Whatcha doin', Grandpa?"

"Oh, I'm working on the tractor."

We play in the manure-filled corral.
Snort, whinny, wet nose searching,
Grandpa's Appaloosa always knows
we've been to the crabapple tree.

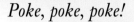

Poke, poke, poke!

We tease the neighbor's pig
until it digs a hole.

Squealing, then snorting, it chases us
through the fields, up the hill,
right through Grandpa's garden.

We scream and run all the way to the house
and stumble in the front door.

Hair in pigtails and wispy braids,
too-short pants, grass stains and dirty knees.
We kick off our shoes and
stomp across the wooden floor.

The walls are covered with photographs of
family and rodeos:
Uncle riding a bucking bronco,
Grandpa's army regiment,
our great-grandparents in the garden
and Yayah, young, with a beautiful smile.

"Grandpa, what was Yayah like?"
We ask because we don't remember.

"She always told funny stories
and she loved to laugh out loud."

We giggle and smile because
when our moms and aunties are together,
they laugh so long and so loud
that sometimes they get the snorts.

There is a big pot cooking on the stove,
and the house smells funny.
Grandpa always tries to feed us weird food.

"Don't want no Rocky Mountain oysters.
Don't want liver or tripe, neither.
Grandpa, where's your candy jar?"

We rummage through the kitchen cupboards
until we find the candy jar.
We suck until our lips turn colors:
red, blue and green.

Grandpa has a secret room.
The lights are always out; the curtains always closed.
Old trunks and wooden boxes line the walls,
dusty and mysterious.

Step, step, step…

We step sneaky steps on tiptoes
across the creaky floor.
Our favorite place to look is inside an old wooden trunk.
It has worn brass handles and wooden drawers.

Lined with blue, it holds
a gold watch, a silver chain, a ring
and a row of ribbons and medals.
Tucked away underneath everything are
black-and-white photos of Grandpa from 1942.
A young man dressed in an army uniform.

Once a soldier, now a veteran, Grandpa is our everything —
elder, gardener, chef, businessman, rancher, cowboy…
But best of all, he's Grandpa.